# The United Nations

# 50th

# Anniversary Book

**by Barbara Brenner**

A Byron Preiss Book

Atheneum Books For Young Readers

**Atheneum Books for Young Readers**

An imprint of Simon & Schuster Children's Publishing Division

1230 Avenue of the Americas

New York, NY 10020

Photographs reproduced by the courtesy of the United Nations; UNESCO: F. Anderson, 54;

Henri Stierlin, 76; UNICEF: Fran Antmann, 82 (C-66: 15); Laurie Bachman, 23 (73-21); Patricio Baeza, 74 (C-85: 12, C-85: 5); Yann Gamblin,

50 (C-1: 1, 8), 51 (C 1: 2, 6, 18); Jeremy Hartley, 61, 84 (C-53: 7); John Isaac, 4 (C-93: 19), 5 (C-93: 2), 31 (C-101: 5, 8, 6), 69 (C-33: 18), 70 (C-93: 12);

Francene Keery, 42 (4731); Roger Lemoyne, 38 (92-148); Peter Magubane, 35 (C-60: 8); Ruby Mera, 3 (17), 4 (27), 23 (73-33), 41 (27); Maggie Murray-

Lee, 47, 49; G. Pirozzi, 5 (C-94: 2), 47 (C-94: 7), 60 (C-94: 4); Shelley Rotner, 2 (C. 4434), 24 (C-47: 5); Schneider, 39 (C-75: 3); J. Schytte, 59 (C-69: 19);

Sean Sprague, 4 (C-64: 4), 22 (C-71: 19), 59 (C-64: 8); C. Watson, 60 (C-39: 3), 61 (C-39: 3);A. Wright 5 (C-48: 3), 66 (C-48: 5), 73 (C-48: 4),

74 (C-48: 9); Zlatko Kalle, 30 (5069); Envision: Sue Pashko, 64; Steve Pace, 37; Jean Higgins, 37; NASA, 78-81;

Naomi Wax, 76; Ramapo High School, 52-53; American Cancer Society 63, 67;

Tony Stone Images (cover).

Art Director: Heidi North

Design Director: Juan Gallardo

Book design by Todd Sutherland.

The text of this book is set in Cheltenham.

Photo research by Cheryl Moch

Manufactured in Mexico

10 9 8 7 6 5 4 3 2 1

Library of Congress Cataloging–in–Publication Data

Brenner, Barbara.

The United Nations 50th anniversary book / by Barbara Brenner. —1st ed.

p.    cm.

Includes index.

ISBN 0–689—31912–6

1. United Nations—Anniversaries, etc.—Juvenile literature.

[1. United Nations.]  I. Title.

JX1977.B69 1995

341.23'1—dc20        94–12784

*To my friend Estelle*

*t*his book was a challenging task which involved, literally, bringing a world of ideas together. It couldn't have been done without a team effort. I'd like to acknowledge the team: There was, first of all, my friend and long-time publishing colleague Byron Preiss, who shared with me his vision of a United Nations book project and who trusted me enough to allow me to help shape it. His staff, most importantly Wendy Wax, my in-house editor, was unflaggingly supportive. Kathy Huck, Vicky Rauhofer, Deborah Valcourt, Hope Innelli, Maria Canal, and, later, designers Heidi North, Todd Sutherland, and Juan Gallardo all helped to move the project forward. I'd like to thank my old friend Gordon Klopf of NGO Action for Children, and Miriam Lyons of that organization. We wish to thank the following people at the United Nations, UNICEF, and UNESCO, who aided us in our research: Rima Bordcosh, Peter Vakhranyov, Jean Ando, Ellen Tolmie, Lisa Adelson, Susan Byng-Clarke, Reynaldo Reyes, Joyce Rosenblum, Vladimir Lubomudrov, Joanna Piucci, Lena Dessin, Goedroen De Vry, and Grev Hunt. A special thanks needs to go to Tom Hinds for offering his expertise. Last but certainly not least, I am indebted to Jon Lanman and Ana Cerro of Atheneum, whose assiduous attention to every detail of this project was an impressive example of publishing at its best.

—Barbara Brenner

# Contents

# The United Nations— a World Family

# Welcome to a Celebration

Something special is happening in 1995. The United Nations (UN) is celebrating its fiftieth anniversary. Actually, it's everyone's celebration. We're all part of the UN. We're connected to it through our nation's membership in the organization. The UN belongs to all of us.

## What the UN is:

The United Nations is made up of many independent nations that have joined together to prevent war, to maintain world peace and security, to develop friendly relations among nations, and to promote social progress. Why? So that more people can have a better life.

## What the UN isn't:

The United Nations isn't a "superpower." Its power comes from the nations that are its members. All together, they make up the UN family—the largest family on our planet.

How many people in your family were alive the year the UN started? (Don't forget grandparents!) Ask your relatives what they remember of that historic event.

---

**The United Nations was officially "born" on October 24, 1945, when its Charter came into force. That's the day that is celebrated every year as United Nations Day.**

---

**Some people say there has been more progress in the world in the fifty years that the UN has been in existence than in the previous two thousand years.**

---

As of 1994, 184 nations belonged to the UN. At the beginning of that year, the UN represented about 5.6 billion people.

# The UN Family
# Connection

"... to practice tolerance and live together in peace with one another as good neighbors ..."

Preamble to the UN Charter

The UN is made up of large and small nations, rich and poor nations, nations that have been in existence for a long time, ... new nations that are just getting started. All these nations are made up of people. So you could say that the UN is ...

## You, Me, Us,

... all connected with one another.

All good people agree,
And all good people say,
All nice people, like Us, are We
And everyone else is They:
But if you cross over the sea,
Instead of the other way,
You may end by (think of it)
Looking on We
As only a sort of They!

(Rudyard Kipling, from "We and They")

Although we may look different from one another, and speak different languages, we have many of the same problems and the same hopes for the future. The United Nations is a way for the world's people to get to know one another, to share our hopes and dreams, and to find solutions to our problems.

# How the Nations Became the United Nations

In 1942 the world was at war. Certainly nothing new. People have been fighting since the beginning of known history, and probably before that. They fight over territory, property, politics, religion, freedom, human rights. Nations fight. Neighbors fight. Even family members fight with one another.

What made World War II different from other wars? It was the second world war in twenty-five years. And it took place in spite of the League of Nations. (After World War I, several nations had formed the League, which was an international organization that was supposed to keep countries from going to war.) Some countries (the U.S. was one) never joined the League of Nations.

When the League of Nations wasn't able to prevent a second world war, it collapsed. At that time, many people said that nations would never be able to work together in a world organization for peace.

Fortunately, some world leaders believed that creating a strong world organization for peace was still possible. Representatives of China, the United Kingdom, the Soviet Union, and the United States—the Allies in World

War II—were determined to form a peacekeeping body to replace the League of Nations. On January 1, 1942, even as World War II was going on, representatives from twenty-six countries met in Washington, D.C., to exchange ideas for a new, stronger international peace organization.

During these talks, President Franklin D. Roosevelt of the United States suggested that the new organization be called "The United Nations."

Forming the new organization took three years of planning. Finally, on June 26, 1945, the United States, Britain, China, France, and the Soviet Union signed the UN Charter. Forty–six other nations, from every region of the world, joined these five in signing, and together they became the founding members of the United Nations.

**Some other world events of 1945: The atomic bomb was used for the first time. World War II ended. Franklin D. Roosevelt died. The Nobel Prize in medicine was given for the discovery of penicillin.**

The fifty-one founding nations were:

Argentina, Australia, Belgium, Bolivia, Brazil, Byelorussian Soviet Socialist Republic, Canada, Chile, China, Colombia, Costa Rica, Cuba, Czechoslovakia, Denmark, Dominican Republic, Ecuador, Egypt, El Salvador, Ethiopia, France, Greece, Guatemala, Haiti, Honduras, India, Iran, Iraq, Lebanon, Liberia, Luxembourg, Mexico, the Netherlands, New Zealand, Nicaragua, Norway, Panama, Paraguay, Peru, Philippines, Poland, Saudi Arabia, South Africa, Syrian Arab Republic, Turkey, Ukrainian Soviet Socialist Republic, Union of Soviet Socialist Republics, United Kingdom of Great Britain and Northern Ireland, United States of America, Uruguay, Venezuela, and Yugoslavia.

# The Preamble to the Charter of the United Nations

The first part of the Charter, the Preamble, lays out the goals of the United Nations.

**WE THE PEOPLES**
**OF THE UNITED NATIONS**
**DETERMINED**

to save succeeding generations from the scourge of war, which twice in our lifetime has brought untold sorrow to mankind, and

to reaffirm faith in fundamental human rights, in the dignity and worth of the human person, in the equal rights of men and women and of nations large and small, and

to establish conditions under which justice and respect for the obligations arising from treaties and other sources of international law can be maintained, and

to promote social progress and better standards of life in larger freedom,

**AND FOR THESE ENDS**

to practice tolerance and live together in peace with one another as good
neighbors, and

to unite our strength to maintain international peace and security, and

to ensure, by the acceptance of principles and the institution of methods,
that armed force shall not be used, save in the common interest, and

to employ international machinery for the promotion of the economic and
social advancement of all peoples,

**HAVE RESOLVED TO
COMBINE OUR EFFORTS TO
ACCOMPLISH THESE AIMS**

Accordingly, our respective Governments, through representatives assembled
in the city of San Francisco, who have exhibited their full powers found to be
in good and due form, have agreed to the present Charter of the United
Nations and do hereby establish an international organization to be known as
the United Nations.

The Charter itself is divided into thirteen Chapters containing 91 parts, called Articles.

# The UN Umbrella

For fifty years peace has been the UN's main goal. But the chapters of the Charter make provision for other important human concerns connected to peace and provide for them under the United Nations umbrella . . .

Disarmament

Disaster Relief

Human Rights

Environment

Development

World Heritage

Decolonization

Education

Health

Children

One of the first official acts of the UN was to set up a program, UNICEF, that would speak to the needs of the world's children.

*1946* The first session of the General Assembly begins in London with delegates from fifty-one member states.

*1947* The General Assembly paves the way for the government of Tel Aviv to establish the state of Israel.

*1948* The Universal Declaration of Human Rights is adopted by the General Assembly. The UN pioneers the concept of peacekeeping observer missions and peacekeeping forces.

*Universal Declaration of Human Rights 1948-1988*

*1949* The UN mediates a cease-fire between India and Pakistan, ending two years of fighting over control of Kashmir. The UN mediates a cease-fire between Israel and the Arab states. UNICEF is established.

*1950* The Security Council calls member states to help South Korea repel the invasion by North Korea (the USSR is absent from the council, protesting the exclusion of the People's Republic of China from the UN).

*1953* The UN coordinates the first global census in history—2.4 billion people are counted. The UN signs a truce with North Korea, ending the conflict with South Korea.

*1955* The UN draws up the first international principles and standards of criminal justice.

*1957* The first African colonies, the Gold Coast and a part of Togoland, gain independence and become the nation of Ghana.

*1959* The UN General Assembly adopts the Declaration on the Rights of the Child.

*1960* UNESCO coordinates aid to move the Egyptian temples at Abu Simbel to higher ground while the Aswan High Dam is being built.

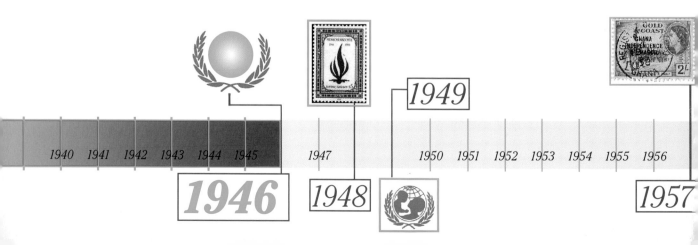

1940 1941 1942 1943 1944 1945    1947    1950 1951 1952 1953 1954 1955 1956

*1946*    *1948*    *1949*    *1957*

*1962* The UN secretary-general plays a key role in resolving U.S.- Soviet conflict over the issue of nuclear missiles in Cuba.

*1963* The UN adopts the first declaration on the elimination of all forms of racism and calls for a voluntary arms embargo against South Africa.

*1964* Having restored law and order, peacekeeping troops withdraw from the Congo (now Zaire).

*1967* The UN helps arrange a settlement of the six-day Arab-Israeli war.

*1970* The General Assembly adopts the first internationally agreed-on set of principles regarding the seabed and the ocean floor as the "common heritage" of humanity.

*1972* The UN Conference on the Human Environment adopts a declaration on the international coordination of environmental issues. UNEP (the United Nations Environmental Programme) is created.

*1973* The Security Council orders a cease-fire in the Middle East war and sends a peacekeeping force to prevent further fighting between Israel and the Arab states.

*1974* The UN maps out the first global strategies to deal with population concerns.

*1975* A UN conference launches the Decade for Women, initiating a major effort on behalf of women's equality. Global environmental conventions on wetlands, waste dumping, and international trade in endangered species are adopted and enter into force. CITES (the Convention on International Trade in Endangered Species of Wild Fauna and Flora) is established.

*1979* The World Health Organization announces that small-pox has been eradicated from all peoples on the earth.

*1980* The World Conservation Strategy, aimed at conserving the planet's living resources, is launched by UNEP, the International Union for Conservation of Nature and Nature Resources, and the World Wildlife Fund.

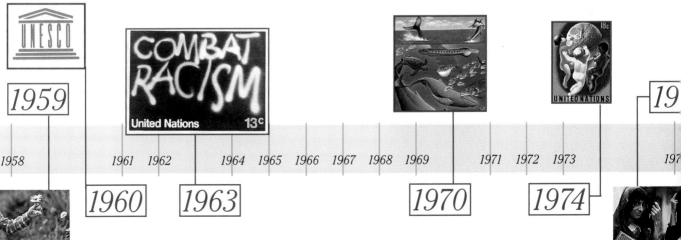

# Key Events in UN History

*1982* The UN adopts the Convention on the Law of the Sea. So far it has been signed by 159 governments.

*1985* The UN adopts the Convention for the Protection of the Ozone Layer.

*1986* Following the Chernobyl nuclear disaster, the Convention on Early Notification of a Nuclear Accident is adopted and enters into force.

*1987* The UN holds the first International Conference on Drug Abuse and Illicit Trafficking.

*1988* The UN mediates the conclusion of the Iran-Iraq war. The UN mediates the withdrawal of Soviet troops from Afghanistan. The World Weather Watch, under WMO (the World Meteorological Organization), celebrates its twenty-fifth anniversary.

*1989* The UN mediates the withdrawal of Cuban troops from Angola and South African troops from Namibia.

*1990* The UN monitors the demobilization of Nicaraguan forces. The UN sponsors the World Summit for Children. The leaders of seventy nations approve a plan to improve the lives of children.

*1991* Operation Desert Storm begins and ends under Security Council guidelines. The Earth Pledge is signed by several world-famous dignitaries, including Secretary-General Javier Pérez de Cuellar. The pledge commits them to act together to improve the earth's environment.

*1992* UNCED (the Conference on Environment and Development)—the Earth Summit—is held in Rio de Janeiro, Brazil. Nations pledge to help one another to preserve the environment through sustainable development.

*1993* The International Treaty on Chemical Weapons is signed.

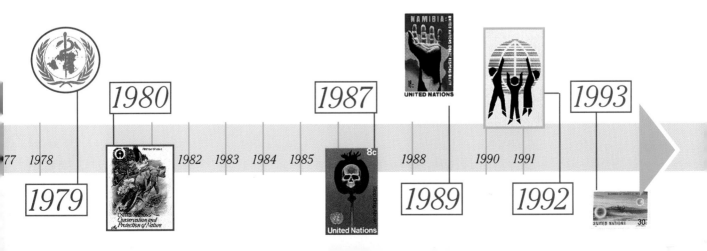

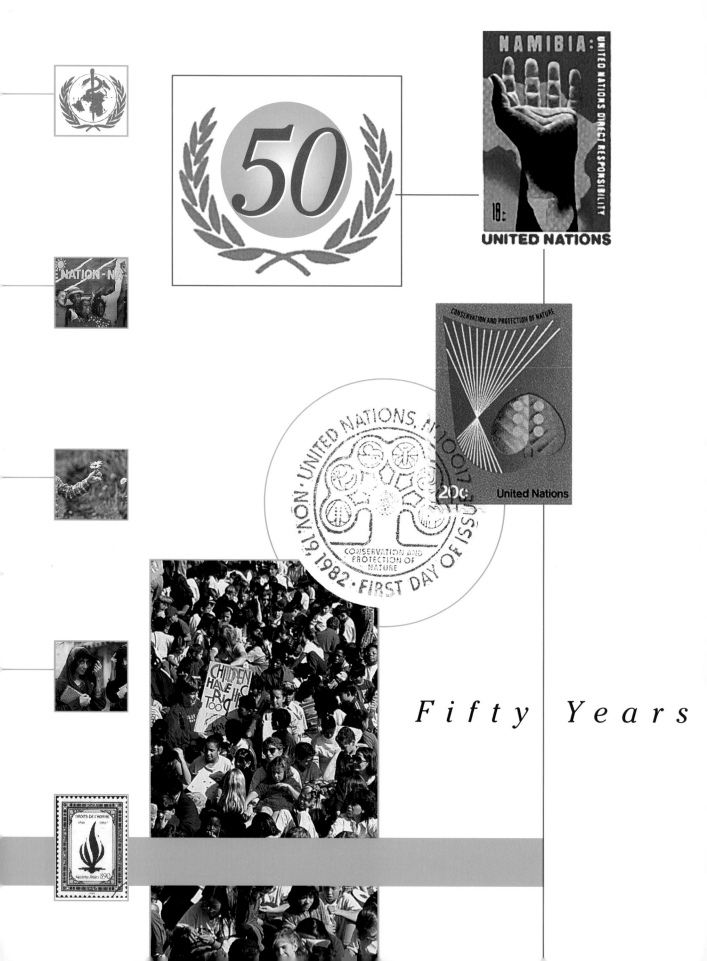

NAMIBIA: UNITED NATIONS DIRECT RESPONSIBILITY

18¢

UNITED NATIONS

CONSERVATION AND PROTECTION OF NATURE

20¢

United Nations

UNITED NATIONS, N.Y. 10017 · NOV. 19, 1982 · FIRST DAY OF ISSUE

CONSERVATION AND PROTECTION OF NATURE

CHILDREN HAVE THE RIGHT TOO!

DROITS DE L'HOMME

*Fifty Years*

# How the UN Works

**W**hat actually happens under that giant umbrella? Where does the action take place? How does it work? The complex and varied work of the UN is carried forward by a network of people of many nations who are all dedicated to one principle of international peace and understanding.

**The General Assembly** is the main body of the UN. Each member nation is represented in the Assembly. Each year from September through December, the General Assembly meets to talk about the world's problems and to exchange ideas about what needs to be done to solve them.

A president of the Assembly is elected each year from among the delegates representing member states.

This is the official UN Headquarters in New York City where the General Assembly meets. The opening day of the General Assembly is the third Tuesday of September—International Peace Day.

Vijaya Pandit of India was the first woman president of the General Assembly. She was elected in 1953.

Like all citizens of a democracy, all member nations of the General Assembly are entitled to one vote, whether they represent a few thousand people or a few million. Many resolutions voted on by the Assembly require only a majority vote, but very important world issues need a two-thirds majority.

Assembly resolutions aren't the same as laws, but they have a great deal of power. A country that doesn't accept an Assembly decision can be made to feel pressure by the other nations. If the country continues to ignore a decision it could, under certain circumstances, even be suspended or expelled from the UN.

The UN General Assembly deals with most of the subjects under the umbrella of the UN Charter.

It also considers and approves the UN budget.

General Assembly meetings use six official languages: Arabic, Chinese, English, French, Russian, and Spanish. As delegates speak, what they say is interpreted instantly into the other five languages. A listener can simply put on a set of earphones and press a switch on the desk or the armrest of the seat to hear an interpretation of what's being said.

People who work at the UN must be fluent in at least one of the six official languages. But the UN encourages all its staff members to be fluent in two working languages. It offers training for that purpose.

**One of the other jobs of the General Assembly is to invite applications of nations that want to join the United Nations. In 1960, seventeen nations became members, the largest number to join in one year since the founding of the UN.**

Arabic
سلام

Chinese
和平

English
PEACE

French
PAIX

Russian
МИР

Spanish
PAZ

Besides its main work in the regular session, the General Assembly also meets with various committees and can call special meetings in other parts of the world.

Representatives of just about every nation or group of people in the world have spoken before the General Assembly.

*Margaret Thatcher (the United Kingdom) (above) and Bishop Desmond Tutu (South Africa) (below) speaking before the General Assembly*

In its fifty years, the work of the General Assembly has grown enormously. At the first meeting of the General Assembly in 1946, there were twenty-nine items on its agenda. In 1993 it dealt with 175 items.

# The UN Design

The General Assembly is the center of United Nations activity. Five councils connect with its work. Think of it as this design:

The Security Council

The Trusteeship Council

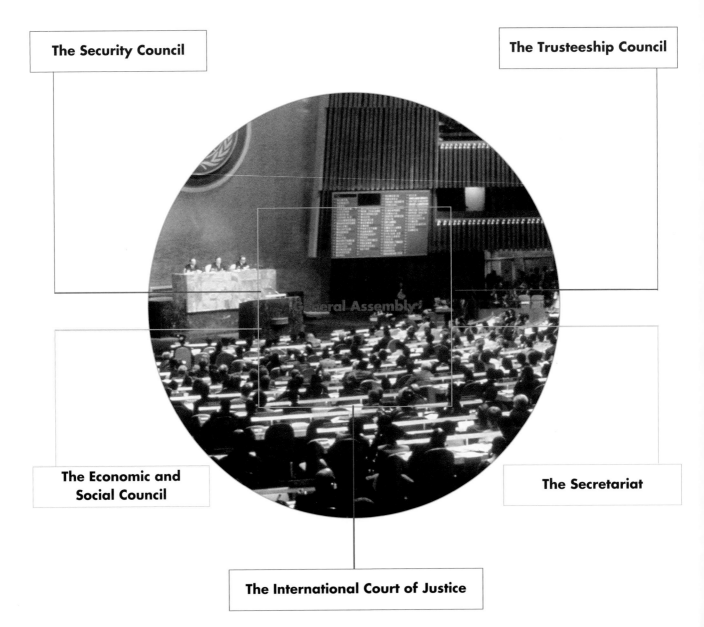

The Economic and
Social Council

The Secretariat

The International Court of Justice

The Security Council is the organ responsible for maintaining world peace and security. The Security Council deals with issues such as disarmament of nuclear weapons. This is the place where disputes and dangers to international peace are aired. Here's where a nation brings a complaint if it's being attacked or threatened.

The Security Council can be called into session at any time as a result of a complaint by a member *or a nonmember*. The Security Council can recommend solutions or terms for a settlement. It's the only body of the UN that has the power to make decisions that the nations involved are bound to accept and carry out.

The Security Council has fifteen members. Five of them—China, France, the Russian Federation, the United Kingdom, and the United States—are permanent. The other ten members are elected by the General Assembly for a two–year term.

Each member has one vote. Most matters require at least nine votes in favor to pass, and all five permanent members have to be among the "yes" votes. If one permanent member uses the "veto," the resolution can't pass, even if there are nine votes for it. Every permanent member has used the veto at one time or another in the UN's fifty–year history.

**In the forty-seven years from 1946 through 1993, the Security Council met a total of 3,323 times. Four hundred and twenty of these meetings took place in the crisis–filled years of 1990 through 1993.**

*The Security Council chamber*

*U.S. president George Bush addresses members of the Security Council*

*The Security Council in session*

The International Court of Justice sits in The Hague, the Netherlands. It acts as the main judicial organ of the UN. It advises the UN on issues of international law and can rule on provisions of such laws. A nation that's not a member of the UN has to obtain special rights to bring cases before the International Court.

One example of the court's work took place in 1984, when the International Court of Justice agreed to hear Nicaragua's suit against the United States for mining its harbors.

*The International Court of Justice in The Hague*

The Trusteeship Council looks out for territories that were colonies and are not yet self-governing. Its goal is to promote a territory's development toward self-government and independence. When the United Nations first came into being, more than half of the present member nations were colonies—regions politically controlled by and dependent on another country. During the past fifty years, the Trusteeship Council of the UN has been instrumental in helping most of these countries gain independence.

**The African nation of Namibia used to be a colony of South Africa. Namibia finally won its independence in 1990, after many years of effort by the Trusteeship Council, UN treaty-making and peacekeeping efforts, and a UN-supervised election.**

The Secretariat staff of more than fourteen thousand people carries out the day-to-day work of the UN all over the world. Some of the staff is based at UN Headquarters in New York. There are also large regional offices in Chile, Thailand, Ethiopia, Switzerland, and Jordan. Employees of the UN are a vast support system for UN work.

The United Nations hires people from all over the world. A person who takes a job with the United Nations pledges to act in the interests of the whole world rather than just in the interests of a particular nation. (UN employees think *globally*.)

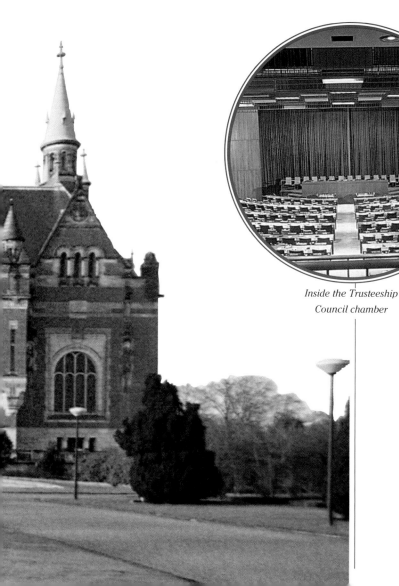

*Inside the Trusteeship Council chamber*

Who pays for the salaries and the running of the Secretariat? Every country pays a minimum, but some countries contribute more based on their national wealth. Currently the United States has agreed to pay one-quarter of the regular UN budget for the Secretariat. That comes to about seventy-eight cents per U.S. citizen per year.

**The Economic and Social Council** operates under the authority of the General Assembly. ECOSOC, as the Council is called, helps set up the programs that the General Assembly votes for. It coordinates the economic and social work of the UN and can study and recommend action related to such issues as development, world trade, human rights, population, education, health, status of women, and other social questions. ECOSOC reports to the General Assembly on its progress. The Council has fifty–four members elected by the General Assembly. Voting is by simple majority, and each member has one vote. One of the important functions of ECOSOC is to work with agencies and organizations inside and outside the UN.

Development is one important aspect of ECOSOC's work. Through the United Nations, countries that have developed, for example, industry, modern agriculture, and educational and health–care systems help countries that are developing those systems.

Agencies and programs of the UN help carry out the decisions of the General Assembly and the work of the Economic and Social Council. There are UN programs and agencies in many different parts of the world.

> **The Secretariat and the agencies together employ more than thirty–one thousand people.**

**FAO** Food and Agriculture Organization. Works to increase output of farmlands, fisheries, and forests. (Rome, Italy)

**UNESCO** UN Educational, Scientific, and Cultural Organization. Promotes literacy. Helps share and preserve cultures. (Paris, France)

**WORLD BANK** Provides loans and assistance to developing countries to help finance reconstruction or development. (Washington, D.C., United States)

**WHO** World Health Organization. Coordinates programs aimed at solving health problems including food, immunization, and sanitation. (Geneva, Switzerland)

**WMO** World Meteorological Organization. Helps world exchange of weather reports. Established World Weather Watch to track global weather conditions. (Geneva, Switzerland)

**UNICEF** United Nations Children's Fund. Provides care of many kinds for children in developing countries. (New York City, United States)

**UNDP** United Nations Development Programme. Coordinates all development activities in UN system. Operates over five thousand projects. (New York City, United States)

**UNEP** United Nations Environmental Programme. Monitors changes in the environment and encourages and coordinates sound environmental practices. (Nairobi, Kenya)

**UNHCR** United Nations High Commissioner for Refugees. Provides food, clothing, and shelter for refugees and helps arrange return to their homelands or coordinates arrangements for their asylum. (Geneva, Switzerland)

**UNFPA** United Nations Fund for Population Activities. Provides aid to governments relating to population and family planning. (New York City, United States)

FAO

WFP

UNESCO

UNFPA

World Bank

UNHCR

These agencies and programs of the UN help carry out the decisions of the General Assembly and the work of the Economic and Social Council.

WHO

UNEP

WMO

UNDP

UNICEF

**WFP** World Food Programme. Provides food to support development activities and in times of emergency. Operates projects in forestry and soil erosion control. (Rome, Italy)

Not all member countries belong to each agency. They pay dues on a separate basis. For example, the U.S. was not a member of UNESCO for several years. And Switzerland, which is not a member of the UN, is active in many UN agencies.

The Secretary-General has the top administrative post in the United Nations. He's secretary of the General Assembly and of the Security Council. He sits in on meetings of the Security Council and can participate in meetings of all UN agencies.

He directs the work of the Secretariat, makes an annual report to the General Assembly, meets the press, and often travels personally to the world's trouble spots to try to make peace.

The candidate for secretary–general is recommended by the Security Council and appointed by the General Assembly to a five-year term. He can be reappointed.

*Trygve Lie (TRIG-VE LEE) of Norway was the first secretary–general. He served until 1952 during the height of the "Cold War" and when UN forces were in Korea.*

*Dag Hammarskjöld (DAG HAMMARSHULD) of Sweden, the second secretary-general, received the Nobel Peace Prize in 1961. He was killed in a plane crash that year while on a peacekeeping mission to the Congo.*

*U Thant (OO TAHNT) of Burma (now Myanmar) served from 1961 to 1966 and then was reelected. He played a key role in resolving the nuclear missile crisis between Cuba and the United States. He was the first Asian to serve as secretary-general.*

*Javier Pérez de Cuellar (HAVIER PERES DAY QUEYAR) of Peru was the first secretary-general from the Americas. He was secretary-general for two terms, from 1982 through 1991, during a time of growing peace between Egypt and Israel.*

*Austrian Kurt Waldheim (KOORT VALDHIME) served from 1972 through 1981, then became president of Austria. During Waldheim's term, the WHO announced that smallpox had been eradicated.*

*Boutros Boutros-Ghali (BOOTROS BOOTROS HAHLEE) is the current secretary-general. His five-year term of office began January 1, 1992. Mr. Boutros-Ghali was formerly deputy prime minister and foreign minister of Egypt. He can speak three of the six official UN languages and is the first secretary-general to come from the continent of Africa and from the Arab world.*

Every secretary-general of the United Nations has added something of his own personality to the work of the UN. When Mr. Boutros-Ghali took office, he outlined some of his hopes and plans for the world organization. He stressed narrowing the gap between rich and poor nations in order to promote peace and security in the whole world. Mr. Boutros-Ghali has said:

*If there is no development without democracy, there can also be no democracy without development.*

**So far, no woman has been secretary-general, but nothing in the Charter prohibits a woman from holding the top UN job.**

# Children and the United Nations

*Children in Algeria*

**A**s a young person, your own connection to the United Nations is very real. From its beginning, the United Nations recognized that children are an important part of the international family. For fifty years it has been representing the needs and the rights of the younger citizens of the world, many of whom have no one else to speak for them.

Can a young person have a voice in the UN? Yes! You don't have to pretend to be a secretary–general or a delegate or someone who works in the Secretariat building. Children of many countries work with the UN.

You can work with the United Nations too. One way to do it is through an NGO. NGO stands for *nongovernmental organization.* That's an organization of citizens of countries. Belonging to an NGO gives you an opportunity to participate directly in some aspect of the UN's work. It will often give you the chance to meet kids from other countries. It's one way to become a direct partner in the work of the United Nations.

*Child expressing her views to an ABC reporter during a children's international congress*

*Global Youth Forum at UN Headquarters in New York*

**NGOs such as the Red Cross, the Girl Scouts, and Amnesty International have chosen to link up with the United Nations to help it carry on its work.** (You can find a list of NGOs on page 88.)

**In November of 1992, 250 kids from forty countries who belong to an NGO called "Kids Meeting Kids," gathered at UNICEF House in New York to meet young people in other countries by long–distance phone. They heard children from Italy talk about the problems of refugees from Yugoslavia. A Mexican boy talked about drug addiction in his country. Brazilians told stories of street children "disappeared" by police. Out of these shared experiences, the kids are making plans to help one another.**

In 1990 a group of children from many nations attended a special meeting of the United Nations in England. Here's a sample of some of the things young people said at that meeting:

"Mr. President, please help the poor so they don't die."

"Please may all children be treated with love and our rights respected just as we respect our grown-ups."

"We children want clean air."

*Member of Kids Meeting Kids reads children's petition sent to world leaders*

All the parts of the UN—the General Assembly, the Security Council, the Economic and Social Council, the International Court, the Secretariat, the various agencies and programs, the diplomats, secretaries, librarians, researchers, specialists, technicians, scientists, educators, writers, linguists, governmental and nongovernmental (NGO) organizations—together form a giant network that helps make the goals of the UN a reality.

Now let's open a window on history and see some of the things the UN has done—and is doing . . . and how you can be part of it.

# The United Nations at Work–
# Yesterday, Today, and Tomorrow

# The Peace Connection

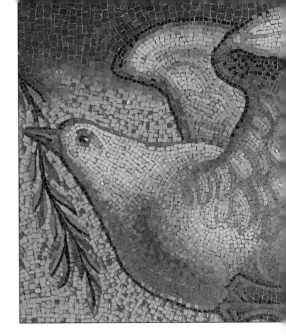

*"The Dove of Peace,"
a gift given to the UN by Pope John Paul II*

**". . . To take effective collective measures for the prevention and removal of threats to the peace . . ."**
UN Charter, Chapter I, Article 1

**W**e've already suggested that the UN is a kind of "family" of nations. Sometimes the family gets along and the members help one another. Other times one member may act like a bully and try to push the others around.

Nations, like individual family members, can get greedy or selfish and want more than a fair share of the world's goods. Sometimes there are conflicts that can't be solved easily by the individual participants. In that case, the UN steps in to help keep peace in the family.

*Boutros Boutros–Ghali, Rohit C. Mehta, president of the International Association of Lions Clubs, and Niken Ayu Murti from Indonesia, the 1993 winner of the club's peace poster contest*

*"Non-Violence," a sculpture given to the UN by the government of Luxembourg*

**Highlight Year 1962**
**Secretary–General**
**U Thant helps resolve**
**world crisis among**
**Cuba, the USSR,**
**and the U.S. over**
**the presence of**
**nuclear missiles**
**in Cuba.**

**1962**

Helping nations to stop fighting has always been the UN's hardest job. Still, in fifty years, it has been able to play a crucial role in the peace process in many parts of the world. For example:

● In the Middle East, the UN's presence helped to lay the groundwork for peace between Israel and Egypt.

● Years of UN–sponsored talks and the personal diplomacy of the secretary–general of the UN brought a cease–fire in the eight-year war between Iran and Iraq.

● In Africa, the Congo's independence from Belgium was followed by a civil war. After more than four years, the United Nations was able to help bring the warring factions together and peace was restored. At its peak, the UN operation in the Congo (now the nation of Zaire) had a force of twenty–six thousand peacekeepers—at that time the largest peace force in the UN's fifty–year history.

The emblem of the UN is a globe surrounded by olive branches, which represent peace. What other design symbols for a UN emblem might have said peace?

Which one of these signs do you think says "peace" the best? Any ideas of your own for a peace symbol?

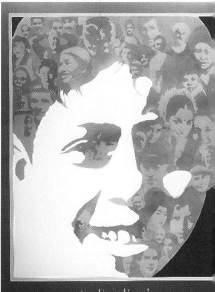

International Year of Peace
Année internationale de la paix
Международный год мира
Año internacional de la Paz

# Peacekeeping: the Blue Helmets

**M**aking peace is only part of the job. Peacekeeping is just as important. Trygve Lie, the first secretary–general of the United Nations, saw this need and in 1948 peace-keeping was added to the UN's functions.

Trygve Lie jokingly called peacekeeping Chapter VI–and–a–half—something between peacefully settling a dispute (Chapter VI in the Charter) and using military force if nego-tiation fails (Chapter VII).

Once peacekeeping became part of the UN's job, member countries volunteered soldiers from their armies to be part of a new international peace team. They wore uniforms and helmets or berets with the blue UN colors. They became known as the Blue Helmets.

*Brigadier General Patil (second from left) and Officer–in–Command of the UN Iran-Iraq Military Observer Group (UNIIMOG) being briefed by* **Hungarian officers** *in Baqubah, Iraq*

UN Iran-Iraq Military Observer
Group (UNIIMOG) supervises cease–fire and
withdrawal of troops to recognized borders

UN peacekeeping forces awarded the
1988 Nobel Peace Prize

There are two kinds of Blue Helmet operations—observer missions and peacekeeping forces.

Observers stay in an area to make sure that cease–fire agreements are being honored. They supervise the withdrawal of troops. They make sure that humanitarian aid is getting to the people it's meant for. They help organize elections and repatriate refugees. Observers often help the peaceful move of a country to independence.

Peacekeeping forces separate the parties to a conflict. They help to decrease tension in tinderbox areas.

**During the first years of UN peacekeeping operations, the Blue Helmets didn't carry any weapons. Now they carry light arms, to be used only for defense.**

UN soldier of the Kenyan Battalion holding a Croatian
child in a predominantly Serbian village

Often their presence improves conditions so that further peace moves can take place.

The Blue Helmets have been doing their work for a half century. In 1994 more than sixty thousand soldiers for peace served in more than a dozen places in the world.

UN soldiers for peace have saved countless lives. And in the process, many have given their own lives in the service of peace. The presence of those blue helmets and blue berets anywhere in the world signifies that the UN has arrived to help peace happen.

*"There is enormous satisfaction when you see progress being made in peace efforts and know that you have played a role—no matter how little—in it."*

Lt. Col. Dermot Earley,
UN Peacekeeping Forces

# You, the UN, and Peace

What does peacemaking and peacekeeping in the world have to do with people your age? Children are the greatest victims of war. More than two hundred thousand children in the world under the age of fifteen are in armies. Most civilians killed and wounded in wars are children.

If countries work together in the UN, the chances of war anywhere are reduced. If people all over the world work at alternatives to fighting, the chances for peace improve everywhere.

In Nanterre, France, a group of kinder-gartners gathered their war toys to form a pile on the classroom floor. They broke them all up and made flowers and other peaceful shapes from them.

You can work for peace in many ways.
You can work globally, through such groups as:

**CHILDREN'S PIECE**
c/o The Children's Peace Coalition for Peace
West-end ISO Building
Social Development Complex
Ateneo de Manila University
Loyola Heights, 1108
Quezon City, Philippines

**KIDS MEETING KIDS**
324 West 96th Street
Basement
New York, NY 10025
United States of America

*Refugee children at school in Croatia, where they learn that tolerance and understanding is essential for peace*

You can work locally by joining a school or neighborhood antiviolence program or workshop in conflict resolution. You can work individually by making peace part of your life.

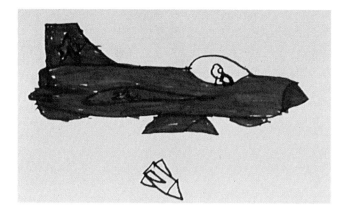

**This is a poem written in 1993 by Edima Suleymanovich, a twelve-year-old girl who wrote it as part of the therapy children in former Yugoslavia are receiving for war trauma.**

A Day in Sarajevo

In my dreams I go among the ruins
of the old part of town
looking for a bit of stale bread.
My mother and I inhale the fumes of
        gunpowder
and imagine it to be the smell of
pies, cakes, and kebab.
Then a shot rings out from a hill
        nearby,
We hurry, although it is 9 o'clock,
and we might be hurrying toward
        "our" grenade.
Then an explosion rings out in the
        street of dignity.
Many people are wounded
sisters, brothers, mothers, fathers.
I reach out and touch a trembling
        injured hand.
        I touch death.
Terrified, I realize: This is not a
        dream.
It is just another day in Sarajevo.

*Children's drawings of war
in former Yugoslavia*

# The Human Rights Connection

Highlight Year 1948
The United Nations adopts Universal Declaration of Human Rights.

*1948*

**"All human beings are born free and equal in dignity and rights."**

UN Universal Declaration of Human Rights, Article 1

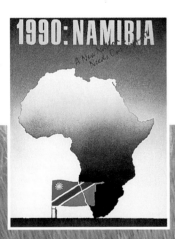

1990: NAMIBIA
A New World Order

For fifty years, the UN has been working to guarantee for all people:

- the right to vote;
- the right to a decent standard of living;
- the right to be free and independent;
- the right to be free from torture or cruel punishment;
- the right to be free from discrimination.

# At Work for Independence

**Target Years
1990–2000
UN Decade for the
Eradication
of Colonialism**

2000

"... to promote ... progressive development towards self–government or independence as may be appropriate to the particular circumstances of each territory and its peoples and the freely expressed wishes of the people concerned ..."

UN Charter, Chapter XII, Article 76

Human rights include the right to be independent— to live in freedom under a government of your choice. When the United Nations was founded in 1945, over half the people in the world didn't have this right. They lived in colonies of other countries.

> **Colonialism is a policy where one nation maintains control over a foreign territory and people. The regions of the United States were once colonies of several nations—Great Britain, France, and Spain.**

> **The UN doesn't decide what form of government a country should have. It helps make sure that the people are free to decide for themselves. One of the goals of the UN is to help colonies become independent nations.**

## In The Gambia

Lamin J. Sise comes from The Gambia, a small country in Africa. He was born in 1944, a year before the UN was founded. At that time his country was a colony of the United Kingdom. He lived under British rule. The British governors decided everything, even what Gambian children learned in school. Lamin Sise remembers that when he was a teenager, the queen of England came to his village on a visit. All the Gambian children were given British flags to wave as the queen passed by. Since it was a colony, The Gambia had no flag of its own.

Lamin Sise remembers the day the first UN teams came to find out what form of government Gambians wanted and to help them attain it. Gambians came from all parts of the country to join in the talks.

The Gambia became a member of the United Nations in 1965. Now Gambians are free to decide what their children will learn in school and how their country will develop. Lamin Sise and all the Gambian people have their independence—and a flag of their own.

OUR FREE NATION - NAMIBIA

## In Namibia

The African country of Namibia had been the responsibility of the United Nations since 1966, although South Africa occupied it. During that time, the UN represented Namibia in international organizations and took legal actions to protect Namibia's interests. It also worked closely with Namibia's liberation movement, the South West Africa People's Organization (SWAPO).

UN efforts finally led to an agreement to insure the independence of Namibia. A specially created UN peace force made sure the elections proceeded fairly and without violence. They saw to it that all military forces were withdrawn from Namibia. On March 21, 1990, the independent nation of Namibia was born.

During the last fifty years, the UN has helped fifty-two countries gain independence from colonial rule. Some people say this has been the greatest transfer of power in human history with the least amount of violence.

At present about 1.5 million people still live in eighteen dependent territories. The largest in area is Western Sahara, which is 103,000 square miles—about the size of Colorado. The largest in population is East Timor. The smallest is Pitcairn Island, which is only a little over a mile square. The administration of all of these territories is overseen by the Trusteeship Council.

# At Work for the
# Rights of All People

"... for fundamental freedoms for all without distinction as to race, sex, language, or religion ..."

UN Charter, Chapter I, Article 1

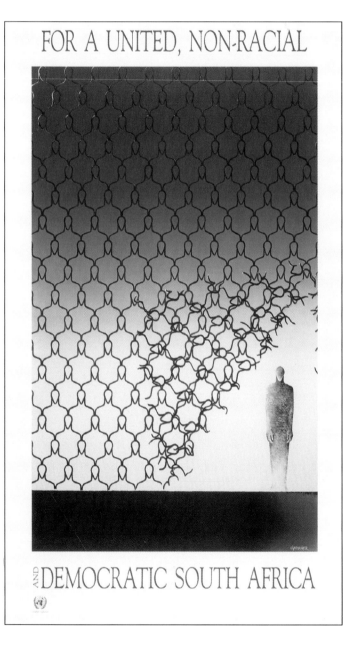

FOR A UNITED, NON-RACIAL

AND DEMOCRATIC SOUTH AFRICA

## South Africa and Apartheid

Apartheid is an Afrikaans word. It means separateness. It's the name the government of South Africa gave to its racial policy. In real–life terms it meant that white and nonwhite South Africans lived on separate land, went to separate schools, had separate bathrooms, and that a white minority ruled over the black majority.

In 1960, sixty–seven demonstrators protesting apartheid were killed in Sharpville, South Africa. The Security Council called on South Africa to stop its violations of human rights. South Africa refused. The UN responded by asking nations to ban South Africa from the international family until it eliminated its racist regime. The General Assembly made resolutions aimed at forcing South Africa to give up its policy of apartheid.

The pressure brought by the UN, including sanctions imposed by other countries, together with the liberation movement of African people, finally brought an end to apartheid. The government of South Africa agreed in 1993 to allow black South Africans equal rights and an equal voice in their country's future. Multiracial elections were held in April 1994.

UN Universal Declaration of
Human Rights, Article 21

*"You can't imagine just how proud I feel to be a descendant, a granddaughter of the Mayan people. Equally, I could be a grandchild of the Aztec people, the Inca people, the Arawa people, or any of the peoples who lived in the Old Continent where I was born. Particularly because here, at the end of the twentieth century, there are many who think that we indigenous people are just a myth, a relic belonging to some time in the past. Sadly, there are very few people in the world who really understand and accept that indigenous people are alive and well, a living people moving towards the future."*

—Rigoberta Menchú

**R**igoberta Menchú Tum is a Quiché Indian from Guatemala. Growing up, she was a victim of discrimination. She couldn't go to school as white and Ladino children did. By the time she was eight years old, she was working on her family's milpa, a tiny plot of land.

Around this time Guatemalan peasants began to press for land reform. The ruling class in her country began killing Indians. As soon as she could, Rigoberta joined her father who was head of the Committee of Peasant Unity, a group that fought for the rights of native Guatemalan people.

When Rigoberta Menchú was twenty–one, her father was burned to death in a fire caused by the police. Her brothers were arrested, tortured, and murdered. In spite of these acts of political terrorism, she continued to be active in political affairs in Guatemala, working to have Indians join fully in their country's political life.

The situation in Guatemala is not fully solved yet. But it is better now than it was before. Part of the reason is Rigoberta Menchú. Because of her work for human rights in her country, Rigoberta Menchú Tum was awarded the UN's UNESCO Prize for Peace Education in 1990, and in 1992 she was given the Nobel Peace Prize.

**The Quiché Indians are the native, or indigenous, people of Guatemala. They are descendants of the ancient Mayans. North American Indians are the indigenous people of the United States.**

# At Work with Refugees

"Everyone has the right to freedom of movement and residence within the borders of each State. Everyone has the right to leave any country, including his own, and to return to his country."

UN Universal Declaration of Human Rights, Article 13

When people don't have a decent life in their country—if there's a war or a famine or a cruel government—they may leave everything behind and run to another place seeking refuge. They become homeless refugees. Today millions of people are refugees, forced to leave the place where they were born and to try to reach a safe place they can call home.

For over fifty years the Office of the UN High Commissioner for Refugees (UNHCR) has been providing emergency relief for refugees. It pays particular attention to the needs of displaced young children.

*Refugees from Kenya*

The UN has helped over a half million refugees to return to Cambodia. In 1988 alone, UNHCR provided services for more than twelve million refugees. It is presently helping the three million refugees who have fled from Afghanistan to Pakistan.

There are roughly 15 million refugees in the world—nine times more than twenty years ago (1973). More than 7 million of them are children.

*Girl stands amid rubble in Iraq*

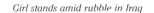

In 1981 the Office of UNHCR received the Nobel Peace Prize.

# Children's Rights

In 1957, the UN made a separate Declaration on the Rights of Children. Thirty years later, the General Assembly adopted the United Nations Convention on the Rights of the Child.

**Principle 1**

All children have the rights written here, no matter what their race, colour, sex, language, religion, political or other opinion, or where they were born or who they were born to.

**Principle 2**

You have the special right to grow up and to develop physically and spiritually in a healthy and normal way, free and with dignity.

**Principle 3**

You have a right to a name and to be a member of a country.

**Principle 4**

You have the right to special care and protection and to good food, housing, and medical services.

**Principle 5**

You have the right to special care if handicapped in any way.

**Principle 6**

You have the right to love and understanding, preferably from parents and family, but from the government where these cannot help.

**Highlight Year 1957**
**UN issues a Declaration**
**on the Rights of the Child**

### Principle 7

You have the right to go to school for free, to play, and to have an equal chance to develop yourself and to learn to be responsible and useful.

### Principle 8

You have the right always to be among the first to get help. Your parents have special responsibilities for your education and guidance.

### Principle 9

You have the right to be protected against cruel acts or exploitation. You shall not be obliged to do work which hinders your development both physically and mentally. You should not work before a minimum age and never when that would hinder your health, and your moral and physical development.

### Principle 10

You should be taught peace, understanding, tolerance, and friendship among all people.

By the end of 1993, 149 countries had signed the Convention on the Rights of the Child. Ecuador was first.

# You, the UN, and Human Rights

In Panama, as part of a program of cooperation between UNICEF and the government, a project for street children and working children includes young people in the planning.

*One of 17,000 children working on the streets of a major city in Paraguay, this boy sells food to passengers on a bus.*

In Brazil, street children created their own organization and went to see the president and members of Parliament to explain their situation and to demand changes in public policies.

In June 1990, 186,000 kids between the ages of six and twelve cast ballots in cities all across Ecuador. They voted for the rights they considered most important for them.

Make a list, with a friend, of the rights each of you enjoy. Check it against the UN list. But keep in mind that many children don't have these rights. Here are a few true stories from different parts of the world. Which rights do these children need to gain?

My name is Maya. I was born . . . in a poor peasant family. . . . I was very happy when I was allowed to go to school. . . . But when I reached the fourth grade, my parents stopped my education. . . . My father said there was no money to pay the fees . . . If I were a boy, my parents would have let me complete school.

My name is Amerigo. I am thirteen years old, and I live on the street alone. Once I worked for an ice cream shop owner. But I got no money in return. . . . I am always hungry, and I don't know where I will sleep the next night. . . .

My name is Gopamma. . . . When I was two, I got sick with polio. . . . I was ill for a long time, and my parents feared I wouldn't survive. I did—but I couldn't walk anymore. . . . Doctors told my parents that if I had been given the polio vaccine in time, I would have been spared the pain. Just imagine, such vaccines cost less than a bottle of soda water!

There are thousands of stories like these in every nation in the world. You can help the UN to help them by joining an organization (NGO) that works with the UN. Here are a few that can help connect you to the fight for human rights:

**Children's Rights Project Assoc. François–Xavier Bagnoud**
129 Barrow Street,
New York, NY 10014
United States

**French Council of Associations for Children's Rights**
6 rue Mathilde Girault
92300 Levallois-Perret
France

**Amnesty International— Children's Urgent Action**
P.O. Box 1270
Nederland, CO 80466
United States

**DCI, Defence for Children International–Columbia**
Aptdo. Aereo 51012
Bogota, Colombia

# The
# Environment
# Connection

**Highlight Year 1972**
**UN Conference on
the Human Environment
is held. UN Environmental
Programme (UNEP) is created.**

*1972*

"To assist Governments and other bodies to promote a better human environment through better development and management of human settlements, and improved technology . . ."

One goal of the United Nations Environmental Programme

**A** rain forest in Brazil, a lake in Russia, a panda in China, a bay in Alaska, the air over Antarctica—they're all part of the world's environment. And it's a small world. What happens to the environment in one part of the world affects us all. Through the UN's agencies and programs, people of many nations help to protect the environment together.

*Indira Gandhi, prime minister of India, addressing the Stockholm conference on the environment*

**UNITED NATIONS ENVIRONMENTAL ORGANIZATIONS**

| | |
|---|---|
| **UNEP** | **United Nations Environmental Programme** |
| **UNDP** | **United Nations Development Programme** |
| **CITES** | **Convention on International Trade in Endangered Species** |
| **UNESCO** | **United Nations Educational, Scientific, and Cultural Organization** |
| **MAB** | **Man and the Biosphere (UNESCO program)** |
| **FAO** | **Food and Agriculture Organization** |

*Rain forest in western Brazil*

# Protecting Animals

*Giant panda, an endangered species from China*

Today between ten thousand and thirty–five thousand animal species become extinct every year. Some are extinct because of the destruction of the places where they live. Others die because they're hunted illegally or captured by smugglers to be sold.

Recently, the skin of a giant panda was offered for sale in China for thirty thousand U.S. dollars.

Authorities in Rwanda (Africa) seized a young lowland gorilla and chimpanzee from a foreigner trying to smuggle them out of the country.

Police in Argentina (South America) discovered a pet dealer with eleven endangered birds for sale in his shop.

Eight elephant tusks taken from baby male elephants were seized at Cochin airport in Kerala (India).

These things really happened. If it weren't for international laws sponsored by the UN, the wildlife criminals would have gotten away. Instead, all of these cases were prosecuted under CITES. So far 118 nations have agreed to honor the laws laid down in CITES.

**Man and the Biosphere (MAB), a UNESCO program, has established biosphere reserves in seventy–one countries.**

# Protecting Our Waters

*Margaret Trudeau holding an "H₂O" sign during a World Water Day walk in Vancouver, Canada*

Oceans cover nearly three–quarters of the earth. Millions of people and other animals depend on the sea for their very lives. Large bodies of water have a great ability to clean themselves. But even the oceans aren't as clean as they used to be. Bays and other coastal waters are especially at risk from pollution.

> **In Japan, a large number of people were poisoned by eating fish from a bay contaminated with mercury discharged from factories.**

Under the UNEP Regional Seas Programmes, 120 countries from ten different regions work together to prevent pollution and to restore the health of the seas. By 1993, 159 governments had signed the Convention on the Law of the Sea. The task remains to get the large nations—the major polluters—to sign.

In the Persian Gulf area, wide areas of mangrove forests and coral reefs have suffered serious damage as a result of the 1991 Gulf War. UNESCO's Intergovernmental Oceanographic Commission investigates such damage, and its scientists try to find solutions.

*Pollution off the coasts of New York and New Jersey as seen from 60,000 feet above sea level*

*Woman and her children drawing water from the village well in the Sao-Domingos region of Guinea Bissau (left)*

*Boy quenching his thirst from a spring near Thimphu, Bhutan (right)*

**People can live forty to fifty days without food, but only four days without water.**

Only about 1 percent of our planet's surface water is fresh (not salty, like the ocean). It's almost impossible to make more water. But water does recycle itself.

Some of the fresh water you drank yesterday may once have been in a cloud, or part of a lake on the other side of the world. So if water anywhere is dirty or polluted, or if there isn't enough of it, it matters to all living things everywhere.

In Brazil, UNEP is helping to finance some of the costs of facilities for flood prevention, sewers, and facilities for disposing of industrial waste.

In Colombia, UNDP has helped forty thousand people living in small communities to get safe drinking water.

UNESCO helps countries to share water—collecting ideas, such as a strip screen, which traps moisture from clouds and mist.

*Children in Guinea Bissau fetching clean water from the village pump*

**March 22 is World Water Day. A hot air balloon, called "The Drop of Hope," was sent into the air above UN Headquarters in New York City on that date in 1993.**

*Women washing at Vridhachalam, India*

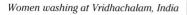

# Clearing the Air

In 1985 scientists discovered a "hole" in the ozone layer of the atmosphere above Antarctica. It was as wide as the United States! Ozone is a gas that shields us from the sun's harmful ultraviolet rays. Chlorofluorocarbons (CFCs) evaporate and break down ozone. Exhaust from cars also affects the ozone.

The UN helps governments reach agreements on how to protect the world's air. The UN treaty called the "Montreal Protocol on Substances that Deplete the Ozone Layer" came into force in 1988. Signers of this treaty agree to stop producing CFCs by the year 2000. Some nations are already stopping, and scientists say that the results are encouraging.

In Dayton, Ohio, a UNESCO program sponsored the planting of grass and trees along busy downtown streets. The experiment not only reduced temperature in the business section, but the trees absorbed carbon dioxide and released oxygen, cleaning the air.

> **CFCs are gases used in refrigerators, air conditioners, aerosol sprays, and plastic containers in fast-food restaurants. They can remain in the atmosphere for as long as three hundred years.**

# Protecting the Land

*In Niger, young boys learn how to cultivate sorghum and rice in their UNICEF–assisted school garden cooperative.*

**S**ome of the world's land is good for growing things. Other land is poor or polluted or shows the effects of drought or war. Sometimes it hasn't been used wisely. Every year up to 6,880,000 acres (17,000,000 hectares) of forest disappear. That's an area bigger than all of Germany!

*Sign in Rio Branco, western Brazil, which means "preserve the environment"*

If too many forests disappear, people, plants, animals, and birds all suffer. Forests help to hold moisture and soil. Land where too many trees have been cut down can turn into a desert where people often can't grow enough food or get enough water.

In Mauritania, shifting sand dunes have left 75 percent of the country a desert. UN teams helped plant vegetation barriers, rebuild dunes, and fence roads.

In Porto-Novo, Benin (Africa), mountains of garbage used to rot in the streets. Through funds from UNDP, organic waste is now collected and used for compost, which is then used by the young people of the community to grow vegetables.

*Women from the town of Kaona, Burkina Faso, terracing the soil to control erosion*

*Agricultural development project organized by villagers and nomadic tribesmen*

> **According to UN figures, one person in an industrialized nation uses 14 to 115 times more paper, 6 to 52 times more meat, and 10 to 35 times more energy than a person in a developing country.**

**Highlight Year 1972**
**UN establishes**
**United Nations Disaster**
**Relief Organization**
**(UNDRO).**

1972

# Protecting Against Environmental
## Disaster

**S**ometimes a natural disaster happens—an earthquake, a hurricane, or the eruption of a volcano. Often, in a case like this, a country's own government and people help. But some disasters are too big for one country to handle. The result of this kind of destruction is an increase in the number of people whose basic needs are not being met, and additional hindrances to a country's development. When that happens, the UN steps in. Through the United Nations Disaster Relief Organization (UNDRO) and with the help of twenty–five scientific and technical specialists, the UN leads international cooperation in disaster relief.

*In Tepitos, Mexico City, children stand in the courtyard of their home surrounded by earthquake destruction.*

For example, in 1987 a major earthquake rocked Ecuador. Several hundred people were killed, and more than fifteen thousand homes were destroyed. When people began to rebuild, UN technical advisers were able to offer suggestions for how to build earthquake–resistant houses made of local materials. The houses turned out to be not only stronger, but cheaper to build.

*At the Plaza Rio de Janeiro, Mexico City, Girl and Boy Scouts participate in the distribution of UNICEF relief bags to disaster victims.*

Many disaster victims are children who don't know how to help themselves. UNICEF is one of the UN programs that provides relief to children.

*Urban service workers in Tepitos clear the streets.*

The United Nations declared the 1990s the International Decade for Natural Disaster Reduction. During this decade, the UN hopes to find ways to permanently reduce the loss of life caused throughout the world by the violent forces of nature. It recognizes that it can't control natural disasters but hopes to stop some of the destruction.

*Safe water and sanitary projects are a priority in the hardest-hit areas.*

*In Tepitos, volunteer nurses distribute halazone water purification tablets and oral rehydration salts (ORS).*

*Damage caused by Colombia's earthquake in 1983 is still visible on many buildings.*

The UN World Food Programme, through FAO, UNICEF, and other UN agencies and programs, has helped supply food in emergency situations throughout the world.

# The World's Worst Environmental Disaster

The term nuclear disaster exists in many different languages. In any language it represents horror. On April 26, 1986, the horror happened at a nuclear plant in the Russian town of Chernobyl. It was not the world's first nuclear accident, but it was by far the worst.

From 1986 to 1990 the Soviet people worked to try to contain the disaster. They spent over nine billion rubles (about 4.7 million U.S. dollars) in health care, decontamination operations, and housing for evacuated persons.

For eighteen and a half miles (thirty kilometers) around Chernobyl, the land became a "dead zone" where nothing could survive. More than five thousand square miles of land was contaminated. Four million people's lives were affected.

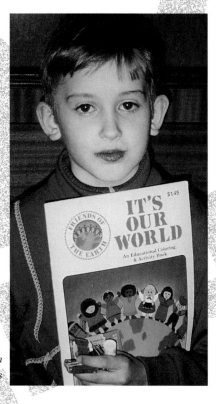

On July 6, 1990, a letter was sent to the secretary–general of the United Nations by the USSR vice–minister of foreign affairs and representatives of Belarus and Ukraine outlining what they were doing and what further help was needed. As a result, more than sixty different international projects were started through IAEA (International Atomic Energy Agency), WHO, UNESCO, UNICEF, UNEP, and other UN and nongovernmental organizations.

*Belarussian boy in hospital receives a
coloring book and crayons*

In 1957 there was a graphite fire at a nuclear plant in Great Britain. In 1979, there was an accident with a nuclear reactor at Three Mile Island, Pa., U.S.

*Two girls dressed in traditional Belarussian costume*

Among them was "Solidarity with the Children of Chernobyl." In cooperation with the World Scouting Movement, more than 1,200 Russian children from the nuclear contamination areas spent a month with families in one of 15 European countries taking part in the operation. Each country welcomed 15 to 150 children.

As terrible as Chernobyl was, it could have been even worse had there been no UN. The UN has become the center of a worldwide effort to help.

There are now more than thirty UN projects going on in Chernobyl and the surrounding areas of Belarus and Ukraine. Many countries are offering money and/or technical help. Housing is being constructed for displaced residents.

Young people of many countries are doing their share. In Spring Valley, New York, U.S., high school students have collected over $10 million for medicines for the children suffering from radiation in Chernobyl. In May 1994 a group of these youngsters visited Belarus and Ukraine to deliver the medications personally. The pictures you see were taken during these visits to the children's hospitals.

*Pytor Kravchanka, the foreign minister of Belarus, is presented with bread, salt, and a pineapple—a traditional Belarussian gift.*

*Students present Pytor Kravchanka with medical supplies for the hospitalized children of Belarus.*

**If you would like to contribute, you can contact:**

## The Ramapo Chernobyl Fund

400 Viola Rd.
Spring Valley, NY 10977
United States

# Children **and the Environment**

Children all over the world are concerned about the environment. With the help of UN agencies and programs, many of them are doing something about it.

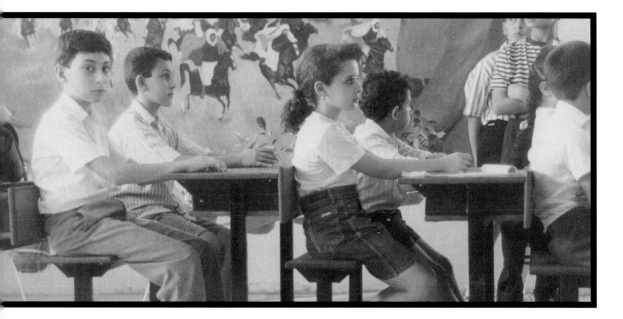

In a seacoast town in Finland, schoolchildren are doing a hands–on study of the Baltic Sea. They're among the thousands of students from 115 schools in nine countries (Denmark, Estonia, Finland, Germany, Latvia, Lithuania, Poland, Russia, Sweden) who are involved in UNESCO's Baltic Sea Project. They're looking at one of the most polluted seas in the world and hoping to figure out ways to save it. Their experiences are being published so that children in schools in other parts of the world can carry out similar projects.

**To find out more about the Baltic Sea Project, contact:**

**Baltic Sea Project Coordinator**
National Agency for Education
Stockholm, Sweden

"The sea is our common mother. We want to see our mother healthy. Now she is sick . . . Decision makers of all Baltic countries you mustn't let our mother die! . . . We haven't inherited this planet from our parents; we have borrowed it from our children."

Children's Manifesto

*Children recycling in Brazil*

**Highlight Year 1992**
**UN Conference on**
**Environment**
**and Development—**
**the "Earth Summit"**

*1992*

### Meanwhile —

In Lamorde, Niger, children are learning to use their land in environmentally sound ways. They grow their own rice and millet in the rainy season and vegetables in the dry season.

In East Kalimantan, Indonesia, local scouts replanted a twelve-hundred-acre forest that had been destroyed in a fire.

At a school in New Jersey, U.S., students campaigned against plastic trays and demanded trays made from recyclable paper. They won. As a result plastic trays were banned throughout their town.

Schoolchildren in Sweden have bought and preserved 160,000 acres (about 65,000 hectares) of forest in Costa Rica with money they made recycling paper and cans.

Over nine million people around the world have signed pledges to act on the Earth Summit's goals.

**Children as well as adults from many nations came to the Earth Summit, and they made their voices heard:**

"The nameless animals who are dying across this planet, I am speaking for them. . . . And we can't afford not to be heard." Severn Suzuki

"It's important for me to ask that politicians are not going to throw my future out the window . . ." Vanessa Sutie

# You, the UN, and Environmental Action

What can you do to help save the planet?
You can do some things on your own.

- Begin to use less paper. Save energy by turning off electric lights when you leave a room.

- Recycle newspapers, bottles, and cans.

- Save endangered animals by refusing to buy or use objects made from fur, ivory, reptile skin, or tortoise shell.

- Plant trees. Use less water.

## Here are some environmental NGOs to contact:

### Global Response
561 Broadway, 6th floor
New York, NY 10012
United States

### National Association of Conservation Districts
East Main, #1102
League City, TX 77573
United States

### Save Our Streams— Izaak Walton League of America
1401 Wilson Boulevard, Level B
Arlington, VA 22209
United States

### World Wildlife Fund
P.O. Box 96220
Washington, DC 20077-7787
United States

You can do even more if you connect with other young people who are interested in the environment. There's power in people working together.

# The Health Connection

> " . . . the United Nations shall promote . . . solutions of international . . . health, and related problems . . . "
>
> UN Charter, Chapter IX, Article 55

**E**arly on, the founding nations of the UN saw the connections between world health, development, and peace.

One of WHO's tasks is to immunize the world's children against disease. Smallpox used to be a widespread and often fatal disease.

Fifty years ago, people were still dying of smallpox. Thanks to the worldwide immunization programs put in place by WHO and other international health organizations, the last case of smallpox anywhere was reported in 1977. The last remaining samples of small-pox virus in the world are in laboratories. They could be destroyed at any time. Smallpox is history!

By 1990 UN agencies such as WHO and UNICEF had immunized 80 percent of the world's children for six major diseases (polio, measles, tuberculosis, diphtheria, whooping cough, and tetanus).

But, surprisingly, many children are still not protected from disease by vaccination. In some countries, children still die of measles, tetanus, and pertussis, or whooping cough.

> **"We have a major problem with immunization in this country; probably less than 50 percent of the adults are current with tetanus and diphtheria boosters."**
>
> The United States Centers for Disease Control

**Highlight Year 1979**
**WHO announces**
**that smallpox has**
**been eradicated**
**all over the world.**

*1979*

More still needs to be done. During a visit to the United Nations in 1993, U.S. President Clinton said, "Just as our own nation has launched new reforms to ensure that every child has adequate health care, we must do more to get basic vaccines and other treatments for curable diseases to children all over the world."

> **The UN estimates that four hundred thousand children have been saved from polio, at a cost of about $10 per child.**

> **WHO distributes bed nets soaked in a pesticide that is harmless to people but deadly for the mosquitoes that carry malaria. Treated bed nets could cut the seasonal death rate from malaria in certain areas by 70 percent. The cost? Only fifty cents per person.**

Of all the killer diseases of young children, one of the worst is diarrhea. It can be caused by drinking contaminated water, or it can result from another disease. Many children could be saved by drinking small amounts of ORS (Oral Rehydration Salts) made from table salt, sugar, baking soda, and potassium chloride dissolved in clean water.

*A nutrition lesson being given to villagers of Ouando, Dahomey*

> **During a recent cholera epidemic in Peru, more than 256,000 Peruvians contracted cholera, one of the diseases that causes diarrhea. With UN supplies of ORS, the fatality rate was reduced to 1 percent.**

# Food for Health and Development

*Guatemalan boy holding a nutritious meal*

In some nations of the world there's plenty of food. In others there isn't enough or people there can't get enough foods that contain protein, which all people need.

In Central America, people get their protein from eating rice and beans. Japanese people eat lots of fish. In other countries they may eat beef, chicken, milk, eggs, cheese—or more unusual (to us) foods, like—termites, iguanas, or grasshoppers. It's all protein!

Food also supplies vitamins. Lack of vitamin A is the leading cause of blindness in children. Vitamin A is found in carrots, squash, spinach, papaya, and other yellow vegetables. UN agencies such as WHO and UNICEF distribute vitamin A supplements to children who need them. Two capsules a year will keep a child from going blind.

The United Nations helps to get nourishment to people who need it. Its first emergency food programs were begun in 1946 in various areas around the world, when the UN was a year old. Since then it has helped supply food in 275 emergency situations in ninety–four countries.

The World Food Programme was started by the UN and FAO in 1963. One of its jobs is providing food to support development. WFP supplies food to families who participate in projects such as building new houses and rehabilitating land.

*Mothers in Zambia cook a maize porridge dish to which sugar is added for the children.*

*A four–year–old girl helps her mother sell red peppers and tomatoes at the all-day market in Bafata in Guinea Bissau.*

In some places in the world people simply have no food of any kind. During several years of famine in Namibia, Africa, an average three–year–old was living on a slice of brown bread and margarine, coffee with half a teaspoon of sugar, and Cremora for breakfast, lunch, and dinner, with dry bread between meals.

> **Kwashiorkor and marasmus are extreme forms of PEM (protein–energy mal-nutrition). It's estimated that between 550 and 800 million people in the developing world suffer from this level of starvation.**

*Guatemalan woman preparing meal*     *Zambian child*     *Namibian child*

Throughout the terrible food shortage, FAO, UNDRO, UNICEF, and other agencies helped to feed thousands of starving Namibians.

Sometimes UN peace forces as well as relief agencies have to be there to make sure that the food is delivered. This was the case in Somalia, Africa, in 1992, when war between Somalians was keeping food from being distributed. UNICEF, UNHCR, UNDRO, FAO, and the Blue Helmets were all there to help the supplies get through.

*Operation Lifeline Sudan, a UN–sponsored massive relief operation, delivers food and other emergency supplies to famine victims in Sudan.*

> **The food that the UN distributes most often is a special emergency food supplement called UNIMIX made from corn, beans, sugar, and oil, along with powdered milk, and high-protein biscuits.**

# The UN at Work for Healthy Choices

**Highlight Year 1991**
General Assembly creates new UN International Drug Control Programme.

*1991*

## Avoiding Drugs

What's one of the worst health choices in the world?

Drugs. Marijuana, cocaine, and heroin are all illegal. Yet more than 40 million people throughout the world are using them. Making and selling drugs has become big business. It has created international terrorism as well as health problems.

**The UN sees drug trafficking as a threat to human beings all over the globe.**

There are a variety of ways to combat drug use. The UN International Drug Control Programme is an international drug prevention network that helps nations to monitor criminal traffic in drugs. But the best way to get rid of the drug problem is to kill the business. If there are no buyers, there will be no sellers. UN agencies and programs help to educate people to make healthier choices by rejecting drugs.

## Avoiding Smoking

Tobacco is a drug.

Smokers and people who live and work around people who smoke are at risk of contracting several respiratory illnesses.

WHO and other UN agencies work on the problem of cigarette smoking on a global level. One thing they've discovered is that the age level when tobacco use starts is moving down. Since about 1988 the number of young people smoking cigarettes has been increasing.

Between 1990 and 1992, three thousand teens started smoking every day in the United States. For every smoker that quits in the U.S. or Europe, two young people start smoking in Latin America or Africa.

How come kids are getting into tobacco at such a great rate? One reason is advertising. The tobacco companies need new markets. They hope to lure children with ads like "Joe Camel" and with ads that try to connect sports and tobacco.

Norway, Finland, Canada, and New Zealand have all banned cigarette ads. In the United States, it's illegal to sell cigarettes to minors. In Nigeria, you can't smoke in any public places.

Three million people a year die from smoking. Over forty thousand studies have shown that smoking is hazardous to your health.

"I must tell you there is no safe way to use tobacco. Tobacco is tobacco is tobacco. Tobacco is dangerous to health—no matter whether it is spit, chewed, or swallowed. . . . Tobacco is the only product that when used as directed, results in death and disability."

Former U.S. Surgeon General Antonia Novello

# Combatting AIDS

**F**ifty years ago, when the UN was founded, AIDS was unknown. Today there are 10 million people worldwide who are infected by the virus that causes this fatal disease.

The majority of its victims are under twenty–five years old. One million of them are children. AIDS is too powerful a disease for one country to tackle alone. The United Nations has helped mount a worldwide fight against AIDS. It is being coordinated by WHO.

Through UNESCO, the United Nations in 1993 created the World Foundation for Research and Prevention of AIDS. The organization investigates new treatments for AIDS and distributes information that helps people to understand AIDS better. Through UN-trained health–care workers and through publications such as the UN book *Facts for Life,* people all over the world are learning that: You can't tell if a person has AIDS by his or her appearance.

AIDS is a virus that can be transmitted from person to person through an exchange of body fluids.

Children can be born with AIDS if their mothers have AIDS.

You can get AIDS from a contaminated syringe or hypodermic needle.

AIDS is most often transmitted as a result of having unprotected sexual intercourse.

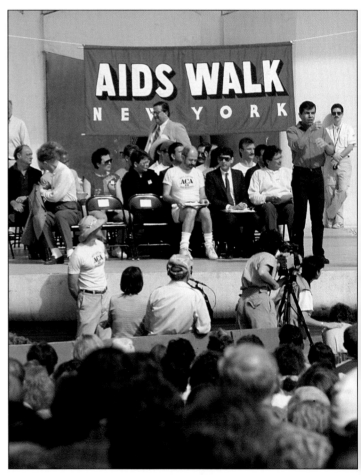

*Crowd listens to speakers at the start of an AIDS walk in New York City*

It's also important to know how AIDS is *not* transmitted. You can't "catch" AIDS from talking to or eating with or being in school with someone with AIDS. Victims of AIDS deserve everyone's help and support.

# The UN, Health, and the Future

**I**n the fifty years since the United Nations was formed, world health education has improved tremendously.

In the Middle East, WHO and UNESCO are cooperating with governments on a joint Health Education Curriculum for 25 million school children.

In China, UNFPA and the All–China Women's Federation run 120,000 parents' schools where parents learn about pregnancy and childbirth, child health, hygiene, and sanitation.

In Colombia, UNDP and teachers organized evening classes for parents to promote children's health and development. By 1989, three hundred thousand parents had participated.

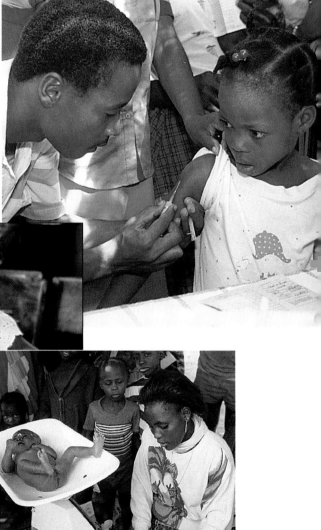

# You, the UN, and World Health

**S**ince the World Summit for Children sponsored by the UN in 1990, many countries have adopted national action programs to protect the health of children. But you and other children of the world are also an important part of the world health education team.

"Help Children Grow" is the name of one global program sponsored by the World Organization of the Scout Movement and the World Association of Girl Guides and Girl Scouts. In Colombia, South America, six thousand Scouts have been trained as health monitors. They help forty-five thousand families protect and promote their children's health by sharing important facts about diet, child care, and hygiene.

"Child–to–Child," started in Britain, now works in sixty–seven countries, helping to spread positive health messages to children and adults. In Mexico, schoolchildren in a Child–to–Child program conducted a door–to–door survey on breast–feeding. They found that the incidence of diarrhea was five times higher in babies who were bottle-fed than in those who were breast–fed. World health experts have found that for the first few months of a baby's life, breast milk alone is the best food and drink for babies.

In Bombay, India, polio immunization went up from 20 percent to 90 percent after schoolchildren were given the responsibility of bringing younger brothers and sisters to the vaccination posts.

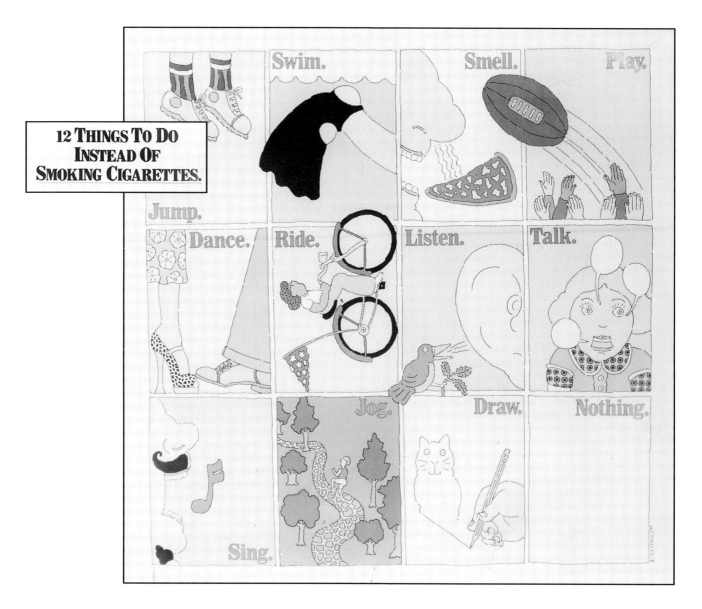

From the U.S. to New Zealand and from Canada to India, local groups have joined with the United Nations to stop the use of tobacco. Nongovernmental organizations of young people, such as the World Scouting Movement and a U.S. group called STAT (Stop Teenage Addiction to Tobacco), are actively helping the UN in its work against the tobacco drug. STAT sponsored a "Kids Don't Smoke" poster contest.

UNICEF and other UN programs have been distributing lifesaving oral rehydration salts in many areas of the world. Often these packets, which cost about twenty–five cents each, are the difference between life and death for a child in the developing world.

You can supply ORS to a child somewhere in the world by sending a donation to:

**CARE**
151 Ellis Street
Atlanta, GA 30303
United States

**Environmental Health Coalition**
1717 Kettner Boulevard, #100
San Diego, CA 92101
United States

# The Education Connection

Highlight Date 1990
International Literacy Year
World Conference on
Education for All.

*1990*

"Everyone has the right to education . . ."
UN Universal Declaration of Human Rights, Article 26

**W**hy is being literate so important? Think about all the things you couldn't do if you didn't know how to read and write.

You couldn't enjoy a book or a letter from a friend. You couldn't read directions or road signs or the instructions on a bottle of medicine. You couldn't figure out how much something costs or if someone were trying to cheat you. You couldn't ever hope to drive a car or get a decent job or help yourself, your family, or your community. There are about one billion adults in the world who can't read or write.

Some nations have laws that you must go to school until you're sixteen years old. Other nations have no laws at all about school.

"The world cheats those who cannot read. " Po Chu–i, A.D. 836

In many places girls are not allowed to become as educated as boys. More than two-thirds of the children of the world who never go to school or who are taken out before completing school are girls.

Education is a step toward a better life for all the world's people. The United Nations works for education through its member countries and through its agencies and programs.

Because of the unrest, revolution, coups, and civil war in Cambodia between 1970 and 1991, education was interrupted. Many adult Cambodians have never learned to read.

In 1961, Cambodia was 80 percent literate. In 1991 only 20 percent of the Cambodian people could read and write.

A project financed by four UN agencies and administered by UNESCO, in partnership with NGOs, is helping Cambodians to rebuild their nation. It has already trained 300 soldiers as literacy instructors. The soldiers will then teach another 6,000 people to read and write.

In Nigeria, one UNESCO–UNDP project helps local governments set up schools for children six to eighteen years old who are nomads. Classes are sometimes held in the shade of a tree by a traveling team of teachers. Across Nigeria there are now 610 of these schools with more than 42,000 students. Many of them have never been to school before.

> **"I know how to spell my own name, but I still have some problems with those of my two children."**
> Cambodian, Chin Chan, age 28

*Classroom in Cambodia*

> **In many countries (Mali, for example), grown-ups must hire people to read aloud to them and to translate articles into the local language.**

**Nomads are people who choose to travel from place to place without a permanent home. The Bedouins of certain parts of the Middle East and North Africa are nomads.**

# Education for
## Peace

One of the terrible side effects of war is the interruption of children's education. The UN helps to start emergency education programs for refugees and homeless victims of wars. The first programs were begun in 1946, right after World War II. UNESCO, in cooperation with local educators, helped set up temporary schools in war-ravaged Eastern Europe. For fifty years the UN has continued to support education for peace.

*Student drawing letters at a calligraphy school in Tokyo, Japan*

*Boy practices his writing at a UNICEF–assisted "drop-in" center for street children in Kabul, Afghanistan*

> **In 1993 there were UN emergency education programs underway in over a dozen countries.**

In Iraq, about fifty-five thousand schools were damaged as a result of the Gulf War in 1991. Children were going to schools that had no water, no toilets, and no supplies. Through a UN inter–agency program, students got pencils, paper, and desks. Local workers received plywood and weatherproofing materials to repair the schools themselves. Eventually four hundred Iraqi classrooms will be repaired and supplied this way.

In El Salvador during the civil war from 1980 to 1992, many families went into hiding in the mountains. The children couldn't go to school. A few local women started schools for the children. There were no books or pencils, so they drew in the dirt with sticks. When peace came to El Salvador in 1991, the UN began helping these teachers and the central government to get together and share ideas for the education of the children of this Central American country.

*Children looking out of an elementary school door in Palung, Nepal*

# Education
# and the Future

Target Year 2000
UN goal of
"education for all"
2000

In the fifty years since the UN was founded, the proportion of children starting school has risen from less than 50 percent to more than 75 percent.

But there's still more to be done. Through the UN, interested teachers from many countries are sharing ideas for creating a world of educated people—the world of which you will be a part.

> In 1966 there were 16 million teachers in the world. Now there are 44 million.

Right now in Zimbabwe, Africa, UN education specialists from UNESCO, UNICEF, and other UN agencies and programs are helping that nation with a project called "education with production." In one school district kids dug a fishpond in the shape of a world map. Through this project they are learning not only about fish farming but also about geography, building techniques, food and nutrition, the environment, marketing, bookkeeping, and the control of waterborne diseases like malaria.

# You, the UN, and Education

How can YOU personally help the UN to make "education for all" by the year 2000 a reality? By staying in school yourself. By sharing what you learn. Get into a tutoring program. Get to know kids from other countries and help them get to know you. Think globally about literacy. Work locally through organizations such as:

**Children's Express**
1440 New York Avenue, NW
Suite 510
Washington, DC 20005
United States

**Street Kids International**
56 Esplanade, Suite 202
Toronto, Ontario MSE 1A7
Canada

There is illiteracy all over the world. A four-year study of U.S. education, released in 1994, said that nearly half of the nation's adult citizens couldn't read or write well enough to write a letter, figure out a bus schedule, or hold a decent job!

Here's the phrase "**education for all**" in six different languages of the world.
Do you know how to say it in a language not shown here?

**Education for All** / English

всеобщее школьное образование / Russian

**Educación para Todos** / Spanish

التعليم للجميع / Arabic

**Education pour Tous** / French

全民教育 / Chinese

# The Culture Connection

**Highlight Year 1946**
UN establishes UNESCO,
the UN Education, Scientific,
and Cultural Organization.

1946

"Everyone has the right freely to participate in the cultural life of the community, to enjoy the arts and to share in scientific advancement and its benefits."

UN Universal Declaration of Human Rights, Article 27

Music. Painting. Stories. Sculpture. Pottery. Baskets. Weavings. Dance. Architecture. They're all part of a people's culture.

The UN promotes the idea that the culture of all people enriches us and should be shared and preserved.

Understanding and appreciating other cultures helps bring people together and furthers the cause of peace.

In the gardens of the permanent headquarters of the UN in New York City, there is a beautiful bronze "peace bell" bought with money collected by Japanese children. It is rung twice a year in a special ceremony.

# The UN at Work in the Arts

The UN, through UNESCO and other programs and agencies, makes it possible for all of us to share the world's culture.

In traditional Africa, a *griot* is a musician and singer who is also a chronicler and historian of the society in which he lives. His art is handed down from father to son. Lamine Konte, a Senegalese griot, plays the kora, a twenty-one-stringed harp-lute made from a gourd called a *calabash.* It produces a sound somewhere between that of a harp and the guitar. Through concerts, records, and publications produced by UNESCO, people all over the world have an opportunity to hear a real griot and to share a musical experience they might otherwise never have.

In 1988, ICOM (International Council of Museums) and the Cultural Heritage Division of UNESCO opened a museum in Libya, one of the first museums of its kind in the Arab world. Now Arab nations can share with the world a culture that goes back to prehistory. Within the first six months of the museum's opening, more than fifty thousand visitors had passed through its doors.

Since 1987 the Swiss Committee for UNICEF has arranged cultural events in elementary schools all over Switzerland. The program is called "Artists for Children" and it brings to children folk music, artists, dancers, and storytellers from various parts of the world.

*Sengalese griot Lamine Konte singing to his own accompaniment on the kora*

"When we go back to our class, children remember the few words the artist taught them in his or her native language; sometimes they remember a song or dance.
. . . And often they want to know more about the part of the world where the artist comes from."

A Swiss teacher

# Saving the World's Heritage

The UN takes an active part in saving the world's cultural and historical treasures. It has helped organize efforts to preserve and restore dozens of buildings and other sites of cultural and historic significance. These places are designated by the UN as World Heritage sites.

Here is one example of the UN's work in this area:

Once upon a time Philae was a sacred island in the Nile river. It was filled with beautiful temples and art treasures of Egyptian culture. Later it held cultural treasures of ancient Greece and Rome as well.

When the first Aswan dam was built in Egypt, in 1902, Philae ended up partly under water, except during the dry season.

As years passed its beautiful ancient temples were eaten away by the water. And then there was talk of another, higher dam. But this time the government of Egypt and scholars throughout the world appealed to the UN to make saving Philae an international project. So in 1960, UNESCO and its member states launched an international campaign to save Philae and the other cultural treasures that were in the path of the dam. Fifty countries made contributions to the UNESCO fund. This made it possible to move all the buildings and artifacts of Philae to the Egyptian island of Agilkia, where they stand today.

*Doge's Palace, Italy*

*Philae's eastern colonnade is surrounded by mud and water.*

*Twentieth–century technology was mobilized to save the heritage of Philae.*

# You, the UN, and World Culture

We each belong to a culture. Yours is made up of the many things you've seen and experienced because of who you are, where you live, who your parents and grandparents are, and where they came from.

One way to find out about your own culture is to interview your parents, grandparents, or other relatives. Ask about songs, stories, family traditions, photos—pieces of the family's past. They're all part of your cultural heritage!

You can learn more about other cultures by visiting a library, museum, or art gallery. Share your culture with other members of the UN family, by writing to:

## Boys and Girls Clubs of America
1318 Regal Crest North East
Calgary, Alberta, T2E 6Y6
Canada

## Creative Response Inc.
952 Lee Highway
Fairfax, VA 22301
United States

## Girl Scouts of the USA
420 Fifth Avenue
New York, NY 10018
United States

> **Children's stories too are part of world culture. The story of Cinderella is found everywhere in the world. More than five hundred versions of the tale are found in Europe alone. The earliest known version is Chinese and dates from around A.D. 800.**

# The Space Connection

**Highlight Year 1959**
**UN adopts first statement**
**on peaceful uses of space**

"This Universe, more vast than all our imagining, and filled with wonders more than we can dream, is a heritage for all mankind."

From *Planetarium*, A Challenge for Educators, published by the UN Office for Outer Space Affairs

**W**hen the United Nations came into being, its goal was to deal with all of the important concerns facing our earth. However, some member nations were already looking beyond Earth—into space.

The first satellite in space—Sputnik—was launched by the Soviet Union in 1957.

With that event many new questions arose for the members of the United Nations. They had to begin to think about a world government that would include cooperation in outer space as well as some international control of its use.

Ever since that time, the United Nations has helped the nations of the world to keep pace with an expanding universe.

# The UN at Work in Space

In 1961, the year that Soviet cosmonaut Yuri Gagarin became the first human to go into space, the UN General Assembly adopted an agreement that space should be used only for the benefit of mankind. Two years later the first treaty banning nuclear weapons in space was put into effect.

The UN developed general principles for the exploration and use of outer space. International agreements and laws were made on the rescue of astronauts, the return of astronauts, and the return of objects launched into outer space.

*Yuri Gagarin*

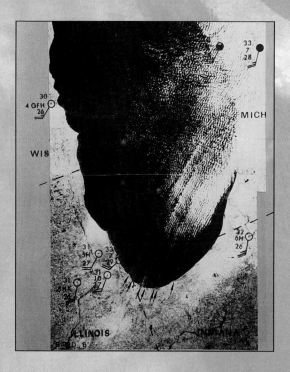

In 1982 the UN held a space conference—UNISPACE 2. As a result, international UN teams began looking at pollution and environmental damage caused by the growing number of rocket launches and the materials they released.

Perhaps one of the most important space agreements made through the UN came into force in 1984. Signing nations agreed that their space exploration to the moon and other celestial bodies would be used only for peaceful purposes.

**In 1975 American and Russian spacecraft linked up above Earth.**

International Space Year was a year dedicated to international cooperation in outer space activities. Since then twenty-six international space projects have been started. Here are some of the things that are being planned or are happening:

Right now, agencies of the UN, in cooperation with the scientists of individual nations, are using satellites to monitor landslides and map earthquake zones. Satellites can act as an early warning system. They can detect volcanic ground swelling and heat buildup. They can watch hurricanes brewing—even predict plagues of insects!

International cooperation is helping countries develop remote sensing data. Satellites can help guide traffic, transmit telephone calls and TV broadcasts, and even see whether countries are living up to their disarmament agreements.

Scientists of the Space Applications Programme of the UN Office for Outer Space Affairs are helping developing countries train their scientists. Plans call for establishing centers in Africa, Latin America and the Caribbean, Asia and the Pacific, and the Middle East. Some of the uses of space technology will be in resources development, disaster relief, and environmental management.

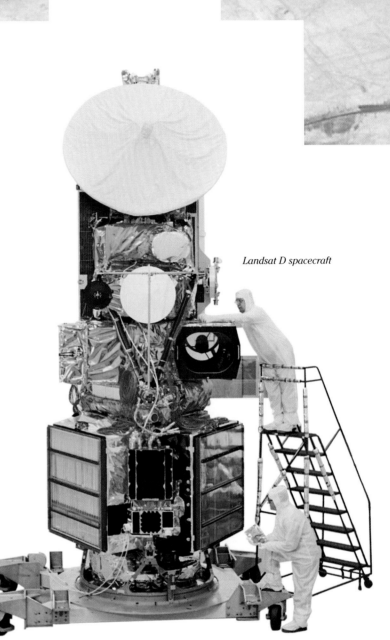

*Landsat D spacecraft*

**The weather and landscape satellite is called Landsat.**

*"One of the central goals of International Space Year is to highlight the importance of understanding the Earth as a single complex interdependent system . . ."*

Secretary-General Boutros Boutros-Ghali, 1992

# You, the UN, and the Future of Space

Space cooperation is the most universal of the UN's accomplishments. But it's up to all of us to help protect space for the future. For example, right now the sky around Earth is threatened by a blanket of light pollution, electromagnetic noise, and space junk.

No clear skies, no astronomy. Which means no star treks. No search for extraterrestrial life forms. No possibilities of space stations. No more opportunities for cooperation among nations in space.

You can help protect space by knowing that:

Air pollution fogs up the sky. It comes from many sources, including aerosol sprays, like hair spray.

Light pollution (reflected light from ground sources) is another culprit. Petition your town to use lights on public buildings that shine down, not up.

*Landsat D model*

Recently a U.S. businessman proposed putting up a permanent billboard in space to advertise his product! Right now, there may be as many as seven thousand objects in orbit around our planet.

Some people have actually suggested that we shoot our garbage into space to save room on Earth. Any plans in your town to use space as a garbage can or an advertising billboard? That's "object" pollution.

"In the U.S. we spend about $2 million a year to light up the sky. Lighting the ground would not only save energy but give us back the stars." David Crawford, International Dark-Sky–Association

# The United Nations at Fifty

# A 50-year Scorecard

**I**n the fifty years since the UN came into being, the world has changed a great deal. Some changes are for the better. Some aren't.

**The Plus Side**

- People now live longer.
- More children go to school.
- The people of the world have more money. (The income of the average family is double what it was fifty years ago.)
- The infant and child death rate is half what it used to be.
- More than half of the world's families now have access to safe water.
- More than two-thirds of the world's people live in independent nations.
- The UN has helped make peace in over seventy places.
- The rights of women and children are being recognized.
- There's cooperation in space.

It's quite an impressive record of accomplishment for fifty years.

**On the other hand, there's . . .**

## The Minus Side

- Nations are still fighting. (There are at least a dozen wars going on right now.)

- Pollution remains a problem.

- The threat of nuclear and other destructive weapons hasn't gone away.

- Issues of race, class, color, and ethnic origin still divide people.

- There are still millions of people who can't read.

- Much more money is spent on arms than on peaceful nation building.

- And—malnutrition and disease still claim 250,000 children a week.

The United Nations has not been able to solve all the world's problems. But it's clear that things would be a great deal worse for all of us if there had been no UN for the past fifty years. It has done what no other organization was ever able to do before. And we know that in the future, the UN will keep on working for peace and justice, for independence and human rights, for a healthier, better life for all of us.

The world needs the UN. And the UN needs you!

> **UN development programs equal $3.2 billion a year. Military spending worldwide equals $800 billion a year.**

# You, the UN, and the Future

**"Children, no longer the objects of charity, are now individuals with rights, who contribute intelligently to society and to good politics. They can inspire our rulers and put them on the right track . . . "**

*Excerpt from a speech by UNICEF Deputy Director Marco Vianello-Chiodo in 1992*

So what can you do?

You can make a difference.

You weren't around fifty years ago.

Now you're a member of the UN family.

You can have a say in what kind of world you'll grow up in.

You can do something every day.

Your own neighborhood is a minimodel of the world neighborhood.

You can support the UN by working locally— for health, for the environment, for human rights . . . for peace.

The UN can only be as strong as the people who support it. Thinking on a world scale and taking action in your own community is the best way to say,

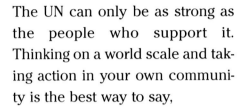

H A P P Y
A N N I V E R S A R Y ,

U N I T E D   N A T I O N S !

**HERE'S TO MANY MORE!**

# Nongovernmental Organizations (NGOs)

**Better World Society**
P.O. Box 96051
Washington, DC 20077
United States

**The Children's Rainforest**
P.O. Box 936
Lewiston, ME 04240
United States

**The Cousteau Society**
870 Greenbriar Circle
Suite 402
Chesapeake, VA 23320
United States

**Environmental Defense Fund**
257 Park Avenue South
New York, NY 10010
United States

**Greenpeace**
1436 U St. NW
Washington, DC 20009
United States

**National Audubon Society**
950 Third Avenue
New York, NY 10022
United States

**National Children's Rights Committee (NCRC)**
P.O. Box 30803
Braamfontein 2017
South Africa

**National Movement of Children**
Higs 703, Bloco "L"
Casa 42
70.000 Brasilia
Brazil

**Project P.E.O.P.L.E.**
P.O. Box 932
Prospect Heights, IL 60070
United States

**The Sierra Club**
730 Polk Street
San Francisco, CA 94109
United States

# Index